OHIO READING CIRCLE BOOK

Grade 6

1980-81

Major Corby
and the Unidentified
Flapping Object

Major Corby
and the Unidentified
Flapping Object

Gene DeWeese

DOUBLEDAY & COMPANY, INC.
GARDEN CITY, N.Y.

ISBN 0-385-13519-x Trade
Library of Congress Catalog Card Number 78–18557
Copyright © 1979 by Gene DeWeese
PRINTED IN THE UNITED STATES OF AMERICA
ALL RIGHTS RESERVED
FIRST EDITION

For my mother, Al: Alfreda
DeWeese, who got me started
reading this kind of thing a lot
of years ago. Thanks for that
and for quite a few other
things.

Contents

*Major Corby
and the Unidentified
Flapping Object*

The ship didn't crash—quite. The emergency systems kept it from smashing into the planet's surface and exploding on the spot, but that was about all.

The observer—the only intelligent life on board—panicked immediately. The ship, of course, told him exactly what was wrong and what material it needed to repair itself, but the information did the observer little good. In the first place, he couldn't understand half the technical terms the ship used. Not only that, he had no idea how to even start looking for the material the ship said it needed. And finally, the ship told him that if the repairs were not made—and made soon—the engines would explode, destroying the ship and everything nearby. Even escape to the planet's surface was impossible, the ship calmly informed him, because the planet's atmosphere would kill him instantly if he so much as touched it, let alone breathed it.

In the end, the observer did the only thing his limited training and the ship's few working systems allowed. He sent out the Collector. And he hoped desperately that it would find a suitable life form before time ran out.

1

"Quit Askin' Stupid Questions and Do Something!"

My name is Russ Nelson, which is short for "Russell," which is a name I'd just as soon never hear again, if you don't mind. I'll probably never get rid of it, though, as long as all kinds of aunts and grandmothers keep coming around and reminding everyone with things like, "My goodness, Russell, how you've grown," which seems to be one of their all-time favorite sets of words.

And that's something else I could do without, all that "how you've grown" stuff. Sometimes I think they're robots and that's all they're programmed for—except grabbing at me, which is another of my least favorite activities. I mean, what do they expect? Fourteen-year-olds normally grow a little now and then, though I guess maybe I overdid it last year when I went from five two to five ten in seven or eight months. I've slowed down since then, only another inch or so in the last few months, but they still all say it, except that sometimes now they also say, "My goodness, Russell, how skinny you've gotten," and someone else will say, "Oh, it's just a stage Russell is going through. He'll start filling out one of these days, you just watch."

"And I'm sure they will. Watch, that is. And then it'll be, "My goodness, Russell, how you've filled out!"

Anyway, all that kind of stuff is one reason I like to get away and visit Corie in the summers. Her whole name is Corie Stratton, and she's the same age as some of my younger aunts, around thirty, but she's a cousin and she doesn't make a big fuss about how much I've grown, like it was the only thing I was able to do or something. Maybe it's because she's about as tall as I am and almost as thin and she went through the same thing a few years ago. Whatever the reason, though, we get along fine. She and Arnie—that's her husband, who's a couple inches shorter and lots of pounds heavier—live out in the country, four or five miles outside Farwell, which is a little town a couple of states away from Milwaukee, and I kind of like it out there. I don't know if I'd like it all year round or anything like that, but for a few weeks now and then, it's great, especially with Corie.

For one thing, Corie's almost always in the middle of another Major Corby story. The Major is a sort of bargain-basement James Bond, Corie says, or maybe a nonbionic Steve Austin, and for the last couple of years, she's been doing a book about him every four months or so. She writes them for a "cheapie paperback outfit in California," which is one of the politer terms she uses whenever they're late with her money, which is at least once every other book.

As for what happened out here at Corie's this summer—well, I wouldn't be at all surprised if her next book is something like "Major Corby and the Sitting Saucer," or maybe "Major Corby and the Unidentified Flapping Object." Whatever she calls it, though, she did threaten to dedicate it to me, along with Cindy and Barlow. And of course the bat.

It all started around midnight that Sunday night, right after I came in on the bus from Milwaukee. Corie had come into Farwell to pick me up, and we only had another mile and a half to go to the house when the car stalled. Corie swore a little, especially when she looked at the gas gauge and saw that it showed empty. That was when I made the mistake of volunteering to take a cross-country shortcut to the house and wake Arnie up so he could bring the other car around with some gas. The first problem was, we stalled right in front of the Saygers place, so that dumb Marvin came charging out, barking his head off. Not that he'd do anything to hurt you, except maybe break your eardrums, but I got over the fence on the other side of the road a little faster than I'd planned. Marvin's as big as a horse, and he could probably do more damage being friendly than a dog-sized dog could do being mean.

Anyway, I was over the fence and heading across the open field toward the woods by the time Marvin made it across his yard and into the road. At least he didn't gallumph over the fence to follow me, which he could've done without half trying. He just kept barking. I guess he was happy as long as nobody tried to get near the house. And Mrs. Saygers, I suppose, was happy, too, peering out of her window to see what Marvin was barking about.

By the time I was halfway to the woods, though, I was beginning to see that a cross-country hike at midnight wasn't the brightest thing I had ever tried. For one thing, the grass was both tall and wet and wasn't doing my shoes and pant legs any good at all. Then, as Marvin's barking faded,

I started hearing crickets and frogs up ahead in the woods, which meant I wasn't going in quite the direction I'd thought. I was probably heading right for the pond, which meant I'd have to detour off to the left to get past the big, swampy area all around it. Not that I believed any of those stories Corie was always telling me about quicksand, not in this part of the country, but I'd just as soon not fool around back there in the dark.

It was about then that I first saw the light. It was just a flicker, way back in the woods somewhere, and it was gone before I could look straight at it. Imagination, I figured when it didn't show up again, or maybe a lightning bug.

Still, it was enough to give me a little shiver, and it did start me wondering what the light would've been if the Major had seen it instead of me. With the Major, it would've definitely been a real light, maybe even an explosion. Or a laser backfiring, if lasers did that sort of thing. And the Major, instead of just being idly curious, would've charged into the woods full tilt to find out what it was. Sort of like Marvin, only the Major didn't bark. That was the way he operated, though. His unofficial motto, according to Corie, was "feet first and hold your nose." No one would get away with it in real life, but, then, if there was one thing the Major wasn't intended to be, it was real.

But then I saw the light again, and this time I'd

been looking right at it, so there wasn't any mistake. It was a light, and it was pretty weird-looking, too.

My first thought was campers, but that didn't last long. This was Barlow Hunneshagen's land, which meant it was private and probably well posted, although I hadn't seen any NO TRESPASSING signs back where I'd hopped over the fence. Or maybe it was Barlow himself. But what would he be doing out here in the middle of the night? True, Barlow turned up at some pretty odd times and places now and then, especially when he'd had a few too many at Chamberlin's or one of the other Farwell taverns, but this was Sunday and they were all closed.

I coasted to a stop a few yards short of the edge of the woods. Moonlight poked through here and there, but mostly I couldn't see a thing.

Then I saw the light again, and this time I got a better look at it. You know what they say about a cold chill running down your spine. Well, one ran down mine and it kept on running, up and down and all over. The light, whatever it was, certainly wasn't a flashlight. It was at least a couple hundred yards back in the woods, and it looked as much like a big, glowing ball as anything. It also looked like it was floating, maybe five or six feet off the ground.

Then the light went away, but the chill didn't.

To tell the truth, I was having trouble deciding whether to panic or to laugh, and all I came up with was a halfhearted chuckle that sounded just plain silly.

But how dangerous could it be? It wasn't as if I was in a city park. People don't get mugged out in the country, and anyway, who ever heard of a mugger with a flashlight? And I *was* getting curious. . . .

I was maybe fifty yards into the woods when the light showed up again. This time I was close enough to see that it wasn't actually being turned on and off but just disappearing whenever it went behind the lower branches of the trees. And it looked less and less like any kind of flashlight I'd ever seen.

My curiosity was fighting a losing battle with that runaway chill when I heard something. It sounded like somebody falling into a bush, and a second later, when I heard someone swearing, I realized that it probably had been. Not only that, I recognized the voice. It was Barlow after all.

"Barlow?" I don't think my voice cracked, but I'm not sure. "Is that you?"

Barlow's voice, sort of raspy and short of breath, yelled back. "Quit askin' stupid questions and *do* somethin'!"

I yelled back with something equally bright, like "Hang on! I'll be there in a second!" Then I really surprised myself by galloping *toward* the sound of his voice—and the light—instead of away from it.

And sure enough, there was Barlow—and, a hundred feet further on, there was the light. And both of them were moving—toward me. Barlow, who looked as skinny and unkempt as ever, was backing up, bumping into trees and bushes and anything else that got in his way. He was also swinging a large stick back and forth in front of him like he was trying to drive something away, which I guess he was.

It was the light he was swinging at, even if it was still fifty feet away, and that's when I got my first really good look at it. The chill came back like you wouldn't believe, along with a batch of other twitchy feelings that I can't exactly describe. The light really *was* a big, glowing ball, a sort of dull, circular glow about six feet across. And it *was* floating, just floating, like—

All of a sudden I felt like exploding, like yelling and shouting all over the place, like those people who go crazy on the game shows when they win a ton of money or a trip to Hawaii or something. I couldn't believe this was really happening, not to me, but there it was, floating in midair right in front of me! This was wilder than anything Corie had ever dreamed up for the Major, and it was really happening—to *me!*

"A flying saucer!" I said in a shaky sort of whisper. "It's a UFO!"

2

"At Least Now It Looks Sorta' Human!"

A UFO, for crying out loud!

A UFO, and of all people, it had to run into Barlow Hunneshagen, who was not only running away from it, he was trying to clobber it with a stick!

"Put down that club!" My voice still wasn't much more than a loud whisper, but it was enough to get Barlow's attention. He jerked like I'd hit him, then whirled around to face me. He had the stick up in the air, ready to swing.

"Barlow! It's me, Russ!"

He blinked a couple of times. "Russ? What are you—" he began, but then broke off and started swinging the stick at the approaching light again.

"No, Barlow!" I managed to yell. "Don't hit it! You'll scare it away!"

"Scare *it* away? That thing . . ." He spluttered to a stop.

I started to say it was probably a flying saucer, but I changed my mind. It would only make things worse, since probably all Barlow knew about saucers was what he'd heard in those scare stories that hit TV every so often, all about smelly monsters and people being picked up and carted away. He just wouldn't understand about other worlds and advanced civilizations and all that.

"It hasn't hurt you, has it?" I asked finally, which wasn't all that brilliant, but it was all I could come up with on the spur of the moment.

"It ain't *caught* me, that's what it ain't!" Barlow yelled. He was still backing up, swinging the stick, and I was having to scramble backwards to keep him from knocking me over.

Then, like it'd been waiting for a cue, the light stopped altogether, maybe fifty feet away. It just hung there, not making a move. I thought I could hear a faint hissing, but maybe it was just a ringing in my ears.

"See?" I said, pointing. "It stopped!" Which was a step in the right direction, at least. Now if I could just figure out how to communicate with it.

Barlow stopped, too. He even quit waving his stick, but he didn't let go of it.

"Just look at it," I went on. "It's just a light, and—"

12

And that's when I took my own advice and *really* looked at it myself. I squinted and looked right into it, inside the glow. There was something in there, I realized, and the more I squinted, the clearer it got and the less sense it made.

The "something" inside the glow looked like— are you ready for this?—it looked like *Major Corby!* Just like on the covers of Corie's books!

"Just a light, huh?" Barlow muttered.

"You see it, too?"

"Silly lookin' guy in a trench coat? That what you see? Yeah, I see him. He's one big improvement, too, let me tell you! It had wings and a tail when I first seen it back there! At least now it looks sorta' human."

Now I started to back away myself. A friendly visit from a UFO was one thing, but a UFO with Major Corby in the middle of it was another kettle of carp altogether. For one thing, the Major didn't exist, even here on earth, so why should he exist out there somewhere? And how would they— whoever "they" were—have found out about him? And why would anyone—or any*thing*—want to imitate him, especially at a time like this? If there was one thing the Major was not, it was a diplomat, so if he was their idea of a goodwill ambassador, then maybe we *were* in trouble.

But then, as we backed away, Barlow still clutching his stick, the Major started to fade.

Some kind of blur was forming and moving around behind him. I squinted again and almost stopped backing away, and the harder I looked, the fuzzier the Major got. Allergic to eye tracks, I thought, remembering one of Corie's favorite comments about anyone who tried to keep out of the public eye.

Then the Major was almost completely transparent, and I remembered what Barlow'd said a few seconds ago. "Wings and a tail," he'd said. Sure enough, there they were. Large black wings showed through the transparent Major, and then a pair of mean-looking, very red eyes. And all the while, the Major continued to fade.

But then, before anything else could happen, a crackling noise came from somewhere near the light, and all of a sudden it started moving away, back the way it had come.

Naturally, I stared like an idiot for a while before I started to follow it at a cautious gallop. Also naturally, I kept stepping in holes and tripping and finally ran into probably the same bush that had gotten Barlow. By then, the light was floating over a small hill, and by the time I made it to the hill myself, it was gone entirely. I was mad that it had gotten away, but I guess I was relieved, too. Anyway, my heart was going like crazy, and that chill was still wandering all over

14

me when Barlow huffed and puffed to a stop beside me.

"Scared it away, huh?" he said between puffs. Now that the thing was gone, he seemed back to normal, except for the heavy breathing. "Thought you said that was your buddy floatin' around in there."

I wasn't paying a lot of attention to Barlow, though. I was mostly coming out of shock and trying to figure out what to do next, whether to run on ahead and get Arnie and the gas or to run back to Corie and tell her what had happened. Arnie and the house first, I decided. That way, I could call the sheriff or someone, and they could get out here almost as soon as we got back to Corie with the gas. And then—

"You all right, son?" Barlow was looking at me squintingly.

"Sure, sure, Barlow, I'm fine. It's just that— Look, why don't you come with me to the house? We can call the sheriff, and you can—"

I was cut off by one of Barlow's patented cackles, which are as close as he ever gets to a laugh. "You're gonna tell *Mel?*"

"Of course. If he gets out here right away with some people, we might still be able to find—"

Another cackle. "Have fun, Russ. But you better do a little thinkin' before you go tellin' Mel you saw a big light floatin' around in the woods, 'specially a big light with a weirdo in a trench coat in the middle."

"What's to think about? We both saw it, whatever it was, and you can back me up!"

"Whoa! Hold up there a minute. *You* can tell Mel whatever you want, but don't go tryin' to drag *me* in on it!"

"What? I don't see— Why *not?* You saw it, too, didn't you? You saw more of it than I did, even. You must've—"

"Like I said, whoa! Just settle down." His face was straight, and his voice was starting to sound serious. "Now listen, Russ," he went on. "In the first place, nobody's gonna believe you. Okay?"

"But *you*—"

"That's the second place. They'd believe *me* even less." He sounded a little sad, like maybe he was sorry nobody would believe him, but then he grinned again. "Besides, there's a third place. I probably won't even believe it myself in the morning."

I shook my head and probably flopped my arms. I tend to do that when I get nervous or frustrated, and if there's anything I was right then, it was nervous and frustrated, especially since I was beginning to get the horrible feeling that Barlow was probably right.

16

"But we both *saw* it!" I said, but it was sort of a last gasp, not a real argument. Barlow just stood there looking at me, and I knew he was right. A patch of moonlight hit his face, and I could see the stubble on his chin and cheeks. He still had a couple days to go till he got his weekly shave. He also looked like he had a few weeks to go before his once-every-three-months haircut. He was a nice old guy—at least he'd always been nice to me, and Corie sort of liked him—but he was right. Nobody'd believe him.

Or me.

"You tell me what it was we seen," he said, "and maybe I'll tell someone I seen it. Okay?"

"Okay," I said. It wasn't okay, of course, but there wasn't much I could do about it. "I probably won't tell anyone. Nobody official, anyway."

"Just your cousin, huh? Thought you'd see it my way." He grinned untidily. "I s'pose I'll be seein' you again, if you're gonna be around for a while."

"Not this year," I said. "I got myself a job, sort of, back in Milwaukee. I have to get back in a week or so."

Talk about "coming down"! A couple of minutes ago, I'd been within spitting distance of a UFO, and now we were talking about a miserable summer job. And the job did have all the earmarks of being miserable. Stuck in some little cubicle of an "office" half the day, phoning people I'd never heard of, asking them questions they didn't really want to answer. Not only that, I was going to have to take a "class" for a couple of days before they'd let me start dialing. Grim. But before you're sixteen, I guess there aren't all that many interesting or well-paying things you can do, legally, so I suppose I should've been glad I'd at least gotten something to make a little extra spending money. Or that's what Dad said, anyway.

Barlow looked a little disappointed, I thought, but his grin popped up again. "Thought maybe I could get a mite more free help with my Christmas trees," he said.

Last summer I'd helped him clear regular trees out of the far corner of the woods so he could plant a batch of pine seedlings this spring. The work hadn't been quite free, but it hadn't cost him a whole lot, either.

"Maybe in the fall," I said, "before school starts again. Maybe I'll be back for a while."

Barlow nodded. "Sure. Come around any time you feel like it." A quick grin. "Just so you don't bring your floatin' friend with you."

And then he was gone, waving cheerily as he vanished into the shadows of the trees.

I stood there after he'd gone, just looking

around, I'm not sure why. Maybe I was expecting —hoping—the light would show up again and give me another crack at it. But it didn't, of course, and I just started feeling all churned up inside again. I had *seen* it! Whether anyone would believe me or not, I had seen it!

I even started wondering if I dared tell Corie about it. She'd make jokes, of course, but at least they'd be friendly ones, not nasty. Still, she believed only what she personally saw with her own eyes, and sometimes she didn't even believe that for very long. And if I told her about the UFO, especially about the Major . . .

I took a last look around, trying to remember exactly where the light had been when I'd first seen it and which direction it had gone when it had disappeared, all of which just stirred up the chill again and made me realize I didn't have the faintest idea what I would've done if the thing *had* stuck around.

Or what I would do if it decided to come back.

I didn't quite run all the rest of the way through the woods, but I didn't waste a lot of time, either.

3

"You Don't Belong to the UFO, Do You?"

I managed to keep the UFO to myself until after Arnie had rescued us and gone grumpily back to bed and Corie and I were alone. Then it all popped out, even the Major.

I have to admit, telling her about it did make me feel better, even if I did feel pretty dumb, especially when I got to the part about the Major.

Corie didn't laugh, not out loud, anyway, but about the time I finished, she motioned me over to the screen door where she'd been standing looking out. She pointed toward the woods, maybe a quarter of a mile away.

"Something like that?" she asked.

All of a sudden nothing seemed silly anymore. There was a light out there toward the woods, and a second later it was gone!

"Yeah," I said, feeling twitchy again, "something like that."

"Didn't look much like the Major to me," Corie said, her long face solemn. "He's usually not that bright, for one thing."

I didn't say anything, but then Corie pushed the screen door open and went outside. The light appeared again and her hand darted out, and I knew right away what it was she'd just pointed out to me. A lightning bug. A feeling of dumbness set in again, but good.

"Still doesn't look like the Major," she said, looking at the bug as it crawled across her now open palm and took off unsteadily. Still looking solemn, she came back into the kitchen. "But if you do run into him again, ask him what he's been up to lately. I've got a deadline in a couple of months, and I still haven't figured out a decent menace for him to knock off."

In the morning, the sun was shining and I could see the woods through my second-floor window. My first thought, once I was awake enough to have one, was that it *hadn't* been a dream, no matter how crazy it sounded, no matter how ordinary the woods looked out there in the sunlight.

It was a little after seven, so Arnie had already

left for his draftsman's job in Bainbridge fifteen miles away, which was just as well. Corie had probably told him about the UFO and all, and I was sure he would have something to say. Compared to Arnie, Corie was downright gullible.

By the time I came down, Corie's portable typewriter was already clattering away in the kitchen.

"Want anything?" she asked as I wandered in.

I knew she wasn't much on fixing breakfast for anyone, even herself, so I rummaged through the refrigerator until I found some milk and a couple slices of ham for a sandwich.

"Going out to look for the Major?" she asked, looking up from the typewriter.

I nodded.

She didn't say anything for a while, but finally she leaned back and said quietly: "You want me to look around with you?"

I almost gave her a fast yes, but I held back. I shook my head. "No, but if I find any saucer parts lying around loose . . ."

She laughed—with me, not at me. "Okay," she said, "it's your saucer."

She glanced at the lamp next to the typewriter. It was one of those little high-intensity jobs, but it wasn't on. "Incidentally," she said, "if you happen to go anywhere near the Engle place, you might see if you can get my wire cutters back. I loaned

22

them to Hal a couple of weeks ago, and now I need them to fix this lamp."

"Okay," I agreed, and then gulped down the last of the milk.

"And give my regards to Cindy," Corie added as I headed for the door. I'm not sure if she smiled or not, but I think she did, at least around the eyes.

I don't know what I was looking for, but whatever it was, I didn't find it. No scorched grass. No saucer parts. No slimy, silvery paths. No mysterious footprints or horrible odors. Not even a note saying your friendly neighborhood UFO had been there last night and would do a return engagement tonight, hopefully with a new cast of characters.

So, after an hour or so, I gave up and headed further back into the woods, more or less toward the southeast, which was, as close as I could remember, the direction the thing had been going when I'd last seen it. I was skirting around the swampy section and was almost to the area I'd helped Barlow in last year when I saw the cat. It was sitting between two rows of the scraggly, two-foot-tall pine trees, licking its front paws single-mindedly.

It looked up when I got within a few feet of it,

and I saw that it was a Siamese. A bedraggled-looking Siamese, at that, or at least as bedraggled as a Siamese could ever get. It looked like it'd just wandered out of the swamp.

"Kitty?"

It quit washing and stared at me with those dumb-looking cross-eyes. There was a collar with an inch or two of leash still attached.

I squatted down a yard or so in front of the animal, and it just kept on looking at me cross-eyed. Then it cocked its head and gave out with one of the more god-awful sounds known to man. I guess, technically, it was a meow! but it was loud enough for a dozen normal cats or maybe a small fire siren. I was glad the beast hadn't been around last night. That kind of noise, UFO or no UFO, would've sent me about ten feet straight up, no questions asked.

"Well, kitty, who belongs to you? With a collar like that, you must belong to somebody." I shook my head and frowned, mostly at myself. People who talk to animals as if they were human were pretty low on my list, and here I was, doing it myself, and it wasn't even my cat. But at least no one was around to hear me. "You don't belong to the UFO, do you? Or Major Corby?" Dumb questions, but what can you say to a cat?

Apparently the cat didn't think much of the

24

conversation either, and it took up its washing routine again. I looked at the collar a little more closely, wondering who the animal really belonged to, and then I started thinking about rewards. I might pick up a few dollars—if I could find out who the cat belonged to. And if I could catch it.

Still feeling like an idiot, I started chatting with the cat again, talking softly and trying to sneak up on it. The cat finally stretched forward and sniffed at my hand, yowled again, and gave one finger a fast lick. It could probably still smell the ham from my sandwich.

Finally it made up its mind. It let out another yowl and ambled toward me. It wouldn't let me pick it up, but after a minute or two of cautious petting, I started walking slowly away, and it followed me. Not like it really wanted to, you understand, but like it didn't have anything better to do.

It was only a few hundred yards to the Engle place, so that's the direction I took. The pine trees ended at a fence a hundred yards behind the house and the other buildings, and that's where the cat suddenly decided to take up sprinting. It streaked under the fence and down the hill, and by the time I made it over the fence, the cat was in the backyard and Cindy Engle was holding it and fingering the remains of the leash. She glanced up in my direction and then disappeared into the house with the cat. So much for the reward, I thought as I made my way down the hill and over another fence.

I waited in the backyard. I knew Cindy'd seen me, and she would be back out when she felt like it. She was sort of like the cat, in a way.

A wire clothesline ran from the house to a shed about forty feet behind the house. A leash several yards long hung from the line, rigged so it would slide along the wire. I was looking at the end of the leash when Cindy came out. She was, as always, wearing a blouse and blue jeans. Her hair, though, was a lot shorter than last winter, almost as short as mine. It looked like she'd bleached it to a sort of brownish blond, but I guess it must've been the sun. Unless she'd changed a lot, she'd never mess around with anything like bleaching.

"Well?" She stood looking at me, her hands on her hips. "What were you doing chasing Wildwood Flower?"

Typical. She likes to put you on the defensive right off the bat, and with me, at least, she's got a pretty easy job of it. I guess I just naturally feel defensive a lot, and Cindy *is* sort of nice—usually. She reminds me of Corie sometimes, which is maybe why I think that.

"You haven't seen me for six months, and that's all you've got to say? What's a 'wildwood flower,' anyway?"

"It's that prize Siamese you were chasing down the hill, and I haven't seen *her* since last night."

"In the first place, I wasn't chasing her," I said. "I just found her out there in the woods. In the second place, what are you doing with a cat like that anyway? And why are you letting it run around loose?"

"I *don't* let her run around loose. *Somebody* cut her leash last night."

"This?" I picked up the loose end of the leash again. "Last night?" The Major and his UFO popped back into my head. Not that they'd ever been very far out of it, but I also suddenly remembered a couple of things I'd seen in the papers last spring, about cattle out on the plains being mysteriously killed and sliced up, maybe by UFOs. I guess I shivered a little and told myself to stop being silly. A UFO with Major Corby in it was dumb enough, but a UFO that went in for twelve-hour catnapping was even dumber.

"Yes, last night," Cindy said. "You know, it came after yesterday afternoon and before this morning. Why? You know something?"

I shook my head, probably too hard. "Not a thing. What happened, anyway?"

She didn't look like she believed me, but she explained anyway. "I had her hooked up out here last night so she could run off a little steam. She was running straight up the walls inside, literally.

Anyway, Mom came out about ten to bring her in, and she was gone. And the leash had been cut. And now it's your turn. What do *you* know about it?"

"What should *I* know? I just got here last night."

"And Flower didn't disappear until last night. Besides, you look guilty."

Unfortunately, she was probably right, at least about me looking guilty. That's just the way I look more often than not, I guess. And whenever I get the least bit nervous, I look like I just got caught trying to sneak into an X-rated movie. I'd often thought of asking Corie for lessons in deadpan, but it's probably not the sort of thing you can learn. You're either born sneaky or you're not.

"What're *you* doing?" Cindy wanted to know when I didn't say anything. "Stonewalling it?"

More like Jello-walling it, I thought, and promptly broke down and told her about the light. Not about the Major, just the light.

When I'd stammered to a stop, Cindy folded her arms and stared at me, making believe she was thinking deep thoughts, while I tried to figure out why I liked her. She was a few months younger than me, but she'd always seemed older. More "in charge," anyway. "Girls mature earlier than boys," she'd said more than once, but I don't think that's all there was to it. It was just Cindy. She was naturally bossy, and she always had been. But at least I was able to talk to her pretty easily, which was more than I could say for most kids, especially girls. And she *was* pretty, I had to admit, tomboy or not. There were times I almost wished she lived in Milwaukee, especially when I had to go to that prehistoric dancing class Mom insists on every so often. And I really do mean prehistoric. One of the first things they tried to teach us was the waltz, for crying out loud! The only trouble was, Cindy'd probably want to lead, and I have enough trouble keeping my feet straight when I *know* where I'm going.

"Okay," she said finally, "I'll let you off this time. Provided you tell me just what you were doing out here at that time of night. Or what you're doing out here at all. Your cousin told me you'd been sold to a telephone sweatshop for the summer."

Trust Corie to have a colorful description. "I was," I said, "but Mom doesn't have to deliver me until next week."

"You don't sound very enthusiastic about your new career. Phoning all those people sounds like fun."

"I suppose it would—to you."

"Is that supposed to be an insult? It sure sounded like it."

I shrugged and managed to not make any

"Mighty Mouth" comments, like I had last time I'd seen her. Instead, I reminded her she still hadn't told me what she was doing with a Siamese out here in the wilderness.

"Wildwood Flower? She's just a loaner. We're taking care of her for someone while they're on vacation. She's a real thoroughbred, or whatever you call cats like that. Papers and everything." She folded her arms again and stared at me. "There are some kittens, too, and I get a 20 per cent commission on any sales I make. Would you or your cousin like a purebred kitten? With papers?"

"They're not housebroken?"

She made a face at me, which I guess I deserved after a crack like that. "Not those kind of papers, and you know it. Well?"

I shook my head. "Not if they're as noisy as Flower."

"That's not noise, that's personality." She shrugged. "Well, you can't win 'em all. Now, what brought you over here? Besides Flower, that is."

"If you must know," I said, trotting out Corie's errand, "I came over to get Corie's wire cutters. You have any idea where your dad has them?"

She looked around. "Last I remember, he was fooling around with something out in the barn. They're probably in with his other tools. Come on, we'll take a look. If you think you'll recognize them." With hardly a glance toward me, she turned and sprinted toward the barn.

She *would* lead, I thought, and then ran after her.

She was shoving the big, sliding barn door open when I caught up with her. The rollers screeched worse than Flower as they scraped along the rail at the top of the door. They didn't sound like they'd been oiled since before I was born.

This part of the barn was just one big room. When the place had been farmed, I guess it had been used to store hay, but now it was empty except for the workbench along one wall. The sun poured in through the door, but the corners of the barn were still sort of dark and shadowy. Cindy trotted over to the bench and reached up to turn on the light that hung over it.

The light came on, a bare bulb a foot or so over her head, and a second later she jumped back. It sounded like she couldn't make up her mind if she wanted to scream or squeak, and all of a sudden my running-up-and-down-and-all-over chill was back, even before I could see what had set her off. I knew she didn't scare easily.

Then I saw it. All I could think about was Barlow's "wings and a tail" remark last night. About two feet from the bulb, just beyond the end of the bench, hanging from one of the horizontal

31

beams that ran along the wall at about head height, was a—a *thing!*

It looked black, and it also looked like it was at least a foot long.

And it was starting to move. . . .

4

"I'd Recognize a Rhinoceros, Too, but That Doesn't Mean I Could Catch One!"

I think saying that I froze just about covers the situation. Cindy probably bumped into me as she backed up, but I'm not really sure, although, under normal circumstances, that's the sort of thing I'd certainly notice. All I could see was the thing, and all I could hear was the faint rustling sound it made as it wiggled around.

Then it started expanding, like a big, black balloon, and I think I would've panicked and run if I'd been able to move. By the time I unfroze, though, I'd realized what the thing was and what it was doing. It was a bat, and it was merely unfolding its wings, although there wasn't anything "mere" about wings like that. After a second or two, the wings twitched and folded back up.

"A bat!" It was sort of a whisper, and I wasn't sure Cindy had even heard me until she said something herself.

"*That* size?" Her voice was higher than usual, but that was better than mine was doing. "Bats don't come that big! Do they?"

"This one does," I said, and then I stumbled backwards as the wings stretched out again, like someone waking up and stretching after a long night's sleep. I didn't *really* expect it to happen, but for a second I could see the wings turning into a cape, and there we would be, facing an upside-down Bela Lugosi, or maybe Christopher Lee.

But the wings folded up again, and this time they stayed folded.

Cindy, I realized, was standing partly behind me, both hands squeezing my arm about the way Barlow had been hanging onto that stick last night. She didn't say anything, and the bat didn't move again, and finally I got up enough nerve to move closer, maybe within a couple of feet or so. At that distance, I could see for sure that I was right. It wasn't really black, but mostly a dark, reddish brown except for the wings. The fur looked short and sleek, almost like Flower's. And the head looked like the head of a tiny, pop-eyed dog, or maybe a fox. It was like a witch doctor

34

had gotten hold of a dog's head and shrunk it down. Very weird looking, to say the least.

"A flying fox," I said finally, "it's just a flying fox."

"A flying what? I thought you said it was a bat."

"It is," I said, and I couldn't help but feel just a smidgen superior, although I didn't think the feeling would hold up for long. "A flying fox is a kind of bat that lives in Australia or somewhere out there."

"Then what's it doing in our barn? For that matter, how do you know what it is?" She was starting to sound more suspicious than scared.

"How should I know what it's doing in your barn? I just identify 'em, I don't explain 'em. And I know what it is because we've got a dozen of them in the Milwaukee zoo."

I twitched a little, remembering the whole herd of them hanging and flapping behind the glass front of their cage. And I remembered something from the information card next to the cage, something about the fact that they always hung out in groups. I looked around the inside of the barn, hoping I didn't spot any more suspicious-looking shadows.

Cindy was leaning forward, peering up at the

creature. "A zoo, huh? It's probably worth some money, then. Right?"

I quit searching the shadows for the rest of the bat herd and looked down at Cindy. "I suppose so. Why?"

"Let's catch it!"

"Catch *that?*"

"Sure. You chicken or something?"

"As a matter of fact, yes." I wasn't too happy admitting I was a coward, but it was better than anything else I could think of. "Even standard-size bats don't thrill me all that much. As for this large, economy-size model— Besides, how could we do it?" Which was, I realized instantly, the wrong thing to ask.

"You tell me," Cindy said. "You're the one who recognized it."

"I'd recognize a rhinoceros, too, but that doesn't mean I could catch one!"

"Don't be silly. That's nowhere near as big as a rhinoceros."

I did my arm-flopping bit. "Look, maybe we'd better just tell your father about it. Where is he?"

"In town. It was his turn to open the drugstore this morning. And Mom's helping him out, if that's your next question."

What I should've done, of course, was ignore her and start back home, or maybe call the nearest

Humane Society. Instead, I found myself actually wondering how I might be able to catch the thing without fainting.

"You got a big sack?" I asked finally. "A *thick* one? And some heavy gloves?"

"Don't go away," Cindy said, and she dashed out of the barn. I wasn't sure if she was talking to me or the bat. Probably both of us.

While I waited, I took a closer look to see what the bat was hanging from, and it turned out to be an electric extension cord that was tacked to the beam. I was nervously unplugging it, trying not to disturb the bat, when Cindy skidded in through the barn door.

"Here," she said, holding out a pair of ragged-looking work gloves and a heavy, white laundry bag. "Will these do?"

The bag didn't look as heavy as I'd have liked, but, then, nothing short of a steel box would've really satisfied me.

"You didn't waste any time," I said. "I was hoping I'd have a little more time to think about all this."

"And let that thing get away?"

I remembered saying almost the same thing to Barlow last night. I was beginning to sympathize with him a lot more.

"We can keep it in that big cat carrier they

brought Flower in," Cindy told me as I put on the gloves as slowly as I could. I kept wondering if I was going to come to my senses before I went ahead and did something really dumb, like actually going through with this. "And even if a zoo doesn't want it," she was going on, "we can always keep it ourselves and charge admission to look at it."

I looked at her, but I didn't say anything.

"Wouldn't *you* pay to see one of these?" she went on. "If you hadn't been spoiled by your big city zoo, that is? Neal will probably want a story about it for the *Tribune*. And a picture. Maybe I can find Dad's Polaroid."

Finally, I couldn't take any more time adjusting the gloves, so I picked up the bag and took a deep breath. "Okay," I said. "Cindy, you get a stick or something so you can poke its feet loose if it won't let go when I get the bag over it."

If I get the bag over it, I thought.

"Won't it let go by itself and fly away? Maybe you should—"

"*You* want to do it?" I held the bag toward her.

She shook her head quickly. "I'm not tall enough."

"I'll get you a chair."

She looked like she wanted to say something else, but she grabbed a screwdriver from the bench and came back and stood next to me.

I opened the bag and moved it up over the bat as slowly and as carefully as I could manage, which was pretty slowly and carefully, considering I kept forgetting to breathe half the time. Finally, only the clawed feet and an inch or so of the legs were sticking out. So far, the bat hadn't made a sound or a move.

Somehow, I got hold of the drawstring and pulled the bag shut, and then I wrapped my other hand around the bag as close to the end as I could without actually touching the bat feet. The thing still hadn't made a sound, and I was beginning to wonder if maybe it had died and was hanging onto the wire only because rigor mortis had set in. It was kind of like waiting for the firecracker you'd stuck under a tin can to go off.

"Okay," I said to Cindy, "see if you can make it let go."

As if waiting for its cue, the bat woke up. There was a sudden thrashing inside the bag, followed by a frantic squealing, mostly from the bat, though I think maybe Cindy and I both contributed a little ourselves. But the claws didn't release their hold. If anything, they just hung on more tightly.

Finally, Cindy recovered enough to jiggle the cord. She even held the screwdriver out at arm's length and tried to pry one of the claws loose, but the creature only seemed to hang on more tightly and squeal more loudly.

Somehow, I made myself grab the bat's legs just outside the bag and pull. All that happened was that the cord started coming loose from where it was tacked to the beam. To tell the truth, I felt like I was coming loose myself. All I could see were the feet, but I could sure feel the rest of it flopping around and hear it squealing. I even started wondering if it could chew its way through the bag.

"Cut the cord," I said. It was lucky I'd already unplugged it.

Cindy stared for a second and then dropped the screwdriver and scrambled around me to the bench. She dug frantically through one of the drawers, found something, and was back next to me in a few seconds, standing on tip toes to reach the cord. Two quick snips, and the bat, still hanging onto several inches of extension cord, slid and flopped the rest of the way into the bag. It was still thrashing and squealing as I pulled the drawstring the rest of the way shut. I let out a shaky breath, and a second or so later, so did Cindy.

Then she held out one of her hands toward me and my bagful of bat. "By the way," she said, her own voice a little shaky, "here's your cousin's wire cutters."

5

"You Two Caught That Thing?"

It took a while, but we finally got the bat, bag and all, into the cat carrier, which Cindy insisted we keep out in the yard, not in the house. "Flower's nervous enough without us bringing in something she'll probably think is a giant mouse or maybe a furry bird. Besides, if it gets away, I'd sooner it got away out here than in the house."

And I couldn't really disagree with her, but the thought of that thing getting away anywhere wasn't all that comforting. For one thing, like I said, bats of any size scare me. For another, this particular bat was probably pretty ticked off at us, and I couldn't really blame it. I'd be ticked off, too, if someone yanked me out of bed in the middle of the night and stuck me in a bag.

Cindy, of course, wondered how I was going to get it out of the bag so she could get a decent picture.

"It'll have to come out sometime," I said.

"Why?"

I had to admit I didn't have the faintest idea, unless maybe it would get hungry and come out to look for something to eat, which only brought up another problem. What were we going to feed it even if it did come out? Cindy suggested Purina Bat Chow, but even if there was such a thing, I didn't think any store in Farwell would carry it.

Finally we decided to do something sensible. We called Corie. At first she sounded suspicious, but it wasn't too hard to convince her that we had *something* she ought to take a look at.

"Okay," she said, "I'll be over in a minute. The Major's trapped in the middle of a blank page anyway, so I'm not getting anything done here."

By the time we got back to the bat, it had managed to find its way out of the bag, don't ask me how or why. Maybe it just didn't like being horizontal. Anyway, the empty bag was laying in the carrier, and the bat was hanging from the wire-mesh lid, looking about the same as it had in the barn. All things considered, it was posing very nicely, but getting decent pictures was another matter altogether. For one thing, the film in her father's Polaroid was black and white, and the bat was pretty close to all black. The carrier and the laundry bag showed up beautifully, but the bat was just a blob.

Corie drove up about when we ran out of film. She gave a low whistle when she got out of the car and saw the bat.

"You two *caught* that thing?" She looked at us like she thought we were a little crazy, which we were, of course, even if Cindy did try to shrug it off like it was something that happened every day. "But now that you've got it," Corie wondered, "what are you going to do with it?"

Cindy explained her plans enthusiastically, all about selling it to a zoo or maybe starting her own local, one-bat zoo and charging admission. I just stood back and listened, like I didn't want to have anything to do with it, which I didn't. Much.

Finally, though, we got all the gee-whiz stuff out of the way, and Corie drove us into town. She was kind of quiet the whole way, tapping her fingers on the steering wheel, and I figured the bat must've sent her off on a new plot for the Major, maybe even something that would get him off that blank page.

In town, Corie parked near the library, which didn't make Cindy all that happy. She wanted to take her pictures right down to the *Tribune* and get the publicity campaign started. "If we wait too long," she protested, "they won't be able to get anything about it in today's paper."

Ignoring the objections, Corie herded us both into the library, although, as it turned out, we might as well have skipped it. All we found were a couple of paragraphs in the encyclopedias and a book on unusual animals. And about all they told us was that the bat belonged to the *Megachiroptera* family, which had wingspreads up to five feet. They said it was also called a fruit bat because it spent most of its time hanging in tropical fruit trees. There was nothing practical, though, like how to take care of one. Since it hung around in tropical fruit trees, it was only logical that it would eat tropical fruit, but nobody said what kind.

At the *Tribune,* though, things went better. Right off the bat, you should excuse the expression, Neal Loftus agreed that the blob in Cindy's Polaroid shots *might* be a bat. Neal's the editor, sort of middle-aged and chatty, and he even agreed to send someone out to take a "real" picture, which choice of words didn't endear him to Cindy. He also said he'd use his WATS line to call all the zoos within a couple hundred miles to see if any of them had lost a bat or wanted a new one.

But best of all, he told us what to feed the creature. "Just pick up a couple of cans of fruit cocktail at the grocery," he said, and when we looked at him a little strangely, he added, "It is a fruit bat, isn't it?"

It was about noon by then, so Corie treated us all to some tacos at a new place that just opened up at the south edge of town. Then she dropped Cindy and me both off at the Engle place and headed back to her typewriter. "I think maybe your bat is going to rescue the Major from that blank page," she said as she drove off.

A little later, Darwin—the photographer from the *Tribune*—showed up and, eventually, got his pictures. He wasn't too happy with them. "Looks like a big black icicle, the way it's got its wings folded up. Don't suppose you could stir it up a little? Or maybe take it out and hold it up for me?" But he apparently wasn't unhappy enough to accept Cindy's offer to hold the bat up for him if *he* would get it out of the carrier and hand it to her. I did slip in a dish of fruit cocktail, though, which was photogenic enough but apparently not to the bat's liking. He ignored it entirely.

About the time Darwin left with his pictures, Corie called and started asking weird questions. Was I in the woods this morning? Did I go anywhere near the road over on the other side? That sort of thing. I kept trying to get a question in sideways, without much luck, but finally she explained anyway. She sounded a little disgusted, but at least it wasn't with me, I realized right away. "It's that Saygers woman," she said, "and Marvin. You remember Marvin."

"I remember I got over the fence last night before he knocked me down."

"Well, Marvin disappeared this morning, and Mrs. Saygers says you took him. She *says* she heard Marvin barking this morning around nine, and she looked out the window and saw you in the field across the road. A little later, Marvin shut up, and she looked out again. You were both gone. And Marvin hasn't come back."

To tell the truth, I wasn't sure what to say. It was such a dumb thing for anyone to think. I mean, even if I'd been there, how was I going to shut Marvin up and take him anywhere? I don't know what kind of dog he is, but he wouldn't shut up for anyone, and he was almost big enough to carry *me* off.

And then, for some reason, I remembered the cat again, and the cut leash. And the UFO, or whatever it was I'd seen last night.

And all of a sudden the thought of the UFO doing a little catnapping—and now dognapping— didn't sound as totally dumb as it had before.

I tried to cut the conversation—inquisition—off as smoothly as I could, but it didn't work. Of course. All it took was a couple of words from me and Corie was sure I was hiding something from her. Like I think I said before, I might as well have a siren go off when I get nervous like that. The results would be the same. She finally let me hang up, though, once I'd promised to be home pretty soon. And after I hung up, there was Cindy. It was like running a verbal obstacle course to get past her without explaining everything, but I finally managed.

And when I went past the cat carrier in the yard, I noticed that the bat still hadn't touched its fruit cocktail.

Corie was waiting for me when I came in the house. She was sitting on the couch, or maybe sprawled is a better word. I leaned against a wall and fidgeted while she explained that Mrs. Saygers had called again to say that Marvin had come back, all soggy and smelly.

"And she's more convinced than ever that you're the culprit," she finished.

"Me? But why? If the dumb dog came back—"

"He came back *after* she called me the first time. She thinks I told you about it, you knew the jig was up, so you let Marvin go. After holding him prisoner somewhere and doing God knows what with him for four or five hours."

"But I was over at Cindy's. You know that. I—"

Corie held up a hand and waved it in a sort of "calm down" motion. "Don't worry about it. That's what I told her. I also told her that if anyone was going to kidnap Marvin as quietly as she said it happened, he'd need a tranquilizer gun and a truck."

I grinned, sort of. She sounded like she was on my side, but she was still looking at me oddly. I tried to think of something to say, but I couldn't. At least I didn't flop my arms, or if I did I don't remember it.

Then Corie was leaning toward me. "I know you didn't kidnap Marvin," she said, "but there's *something* on your mind."

See? What did I tell you? A red light and a siren wouldn't do any better, and it's been like that ever since I can remember. Once Mom accidentally gave me a five-dollar bill instead of a one for my allowance. I hadn't had it in my pocket more'n a few seconds before she and Dad were both looking at me and asking what was wrong, and there went the four bucks.

So I told Corie about the cat and the cut leash and everything. When I rambled to a stop, I could see that she wasn't laughing like I'd expected. In fact, she wasn't even grinning. She almost looked like she was taking the idea seriously, which was the one thing I hadn't been expecting. I stared at her for a few seconds and then did one of my arm-flopping bits.

"Well, that's about it," I said.

She was quiet another few seconds, and then said: "And you think there's a connection between whatever it was you and Barlow saw last night and the disappearing cat and Marvin?"

Another arm-flopping number, and I stuck my hands in my pockets and fell backwards onto the sofa, scrunching into the corner opposite where Corie was sitting. "I didn't say there *was* a connection," I said. "I just said *maybe.*"

"So why would a UFO snatch up animals and then let them go a few hours later?" she asked.

"How should I know? They're supposed to pick people up now and then, if you can believe all the stories, so why not animals? But what difference does it make? You don't believe in UFOs or anything like that anyway."

She was quiet for a few seconds, looking at me. "I don't 'believe in' UFOs any more than I 'believe in' ghosts or ESP or anything else like that. On the other hand, I've never said that all of those things were downright impossible, now have I?" Her face was straight except for the crinkling around her eyes. I know people say you can't smile

49

with only your eyes, but they don't know Corie, that's all.

Anyway, I tried to remember just what she *had* said all those other times, and after a minute I realized she was right. She'd made jokes and she'd come on pretty strong whenever some weirdo tried to convince her that *his* belief was the *only* belief and that if she didn't accept it pretty fast, she was doomed to eternal torture, or at least to eternal stupidity. But she'd never made a flat statement that all such beliefs were ridiculous. Or that all UFOs were hoaxes or hallucinations.

So, we spent the next hour talking about UFOs and spirits and marsh gas and a hundred other things I'd either never heard of or had forgotten. In a way, it was like getting to know Corie—*really* know her—for the first time, and finding out that she was a lot like me. Or I was a lot like her, I suppose I should say. Anyway, we were a lot alike. Neither one of us accepted things blindly, but we wouldn't come right out and say that something was just plain impossible, either. Which makes us either open-minded or wishy-washy, depending on your viewpoint.

When it was all over, of course, we hadn't come to any conclusions, just a lot of maybes. Like, for instance, maybe I had been half asleep last night and I'd imagined the whole thing. "Forest hypnosis" instead of highway hypnosis.

Or maybe there really was something floating around out there in the woods. Something that could look like anything it wanted to look like, even the Major, or a demon.

Or maybe even—if Mrs. Saygers hadn't been imagining things this morning—like me.

6

"From What I Hear, They Travel in Flocks."

Arnie—he hated "Arnold" the same way I hated "Russell"—got a good laugh out of the whole thing, especially the part about Marvin coming back soaking wet and smelling bad.

"It's about time someone dowsed that beast with some ammonia water or whatever. The way he comes charging out at every car that goes by, I'm surprised he hasn't gotten killed or caused a wreck years ago."

"I take it you don't think it had anything to do with a UFO," Corie said.

"Come on, be serious!"

Corie shrugged. "Just thought I'd check."

Needless to say, I didn't feel like arguing with Arnie, so that was pretty much the last word on the subject, and we settled down for an hour or so of Arnie's oddball varieties of chess. For instance, he really likes atomic chess. It's just like regular chess except you have a choice of either moving or exploding a piece. If you explode it, it destroys itself and all adjacent pieces, friend and enemy alike. Arnie says he doesn't have the patience for regular chess, and I have to admit, playing with rules like that sure speeds the game up.

We were finishing our fifth or sixth game when we heard a commotion in the yard. Corie, who had been kibitzing and laughing a lot as she watched our kamikaze strategy, went to the door, and a second later, Homer and Alice Diefenbacher, who lived about a mile down the road, clumped into the kitchen. Homer, who's sort of round and fiftyish, was messier than I'd ever seen him, and Alice wasn't much better. Hair mussed, smudges on their faces, clothes a little off center. Alice was talking a mile a minute and not making much sense. Homer was just trying to shush her. Finally, Corie managed to get a grip on Alice and drag her away to the living room, leaving Homer with Arnie and me.

Homer breathed a huge sigh of relief. "The woman's gone off the deep end, I swear," he muttered, and then looked at Arnie. "You know what she did? Do you have any idea? Of course you don't! You couldn't! Nobody in their right mind—

You want to know what she did? What she did—
We were drivin' down the road, just down by the
corner, and all of a sudden she starts yellin', 'Aunt
May! It's Aunt May!' And then she grabs my arm!
While I'm drivin', mind you! Well, next thing I
know, we're in the ditch! Spang up against a tree!
And she's still yammerin' about Aunt May! Aunt
May! I swear, I don't know what's got into her. I
mean, whose *funeral* does she think we went to
last month if it wasn't Aunt May's?"

All of a sudden he stopped, like his spring had
broken. He sighed again, only this time it wasn't in
relief. He glanced around, kind of like he was
waking up, and he looked at Arnie again. "Mind if
I use your phone? I don't s'pose there's any way of
gettin' around callin' the sheriff."

Corie was the first one to make the connection
between my UFO and the accident. She'd finally
gotten Alice more or less calmed down by the time
I came into the living room where they were still
sitting.

"What, exactly, did it look like?" Corie was asking.

"Exactly like Aunt May, I told you. Just like I
remembered her that last time we were up there.
She was sitting in that old rocking chair she's had

forever and a day, the creaky old thing. She was just sitting there, with a—a kind of halo all around her."

"Halo?" Corie, who must've heard me come in the room, gave me a quick glance. "A glow, you mean, Alice? A light?"

Alice just nodded.

"Did she do anything?" Corie asked. "Did she move around at all?"

Alice shook her head. "She just sat there. Maybe she was rocking back and forth like she always did, but that was all." She swallowed loudly and dabbed at her eyes.

"She was just sitting there at the side of the road? Down in the ditch?"

"Oh, no, not down there!" The words made it sound like Alice was wrinkling her nose at the very thought. "She was up higher than I was. I had to look up at her."

"She was floating, you mean?"

Alice looked puzzled for a second. "Yes, I suppose she was. I just hadn't thought about it, you know. But she must have been."

And that's when *I* finally made the connection. From the questions Corie'd been asking, though, she must've figured it out quite a while ago. It was my UFO again, what else? Only this time it had been floating around with someone in it who was dead instead of someone who didn't exist at all. I was having trouble keeping from exploding, of course, but somehow I managed, especially after Corie gave me one of her looks. And then the sheriff, Mel Kochenderfer, showed up, and we all hustled out to meet him. While Homer gave Sheriff K a much censored version of what had happened, Arnie gave me one of his "keep it buttoned, Russ!" looks. I was getting it from all sides.

Sheriff K groaned when Homer finished talking. "Now why'd you go and do something like that? You haven't been drinking, have you, Homer?"

Homer shook his head vigorously. "Some animal ran out in front of me, that's all," he said.

We were all sort of surprised when the sheriff laughed and then gave *me* a funny look. Not Homer, but me. "What kind of animal, Homer?" he asked, but he was still looking at me.

Homer stuttered but finally said it "looked like a dog."

"You sure it wasn't a big bat? I hear we been invaded by giant bats."

Then he leaned toward me. "Neal told me about that critter you and the Engle girl caught this morning. You don't have any more like that around, do you?" He was grinning, but he was also looking suspicious, or maybe mean would be a better word. I'd heard Corie say she'd never liked him, and I was starting to see why.

I shook my head. "That's the only one."

"No idea where it came from?"

"Not unless it escaped from a zoo somewhere."

"Neal tells me there aren't any zoos like that closer'n a hundred miles. Think one of them things could make it that far?"

I shrugged but didn't say anything.

"Be pretty easy if it took a bus, though, don't you think?" he asked.

I almost laughed when I realized what he was driving at. I thought of a couple of smart answers about batmobiles and smuggling bats over state lines, but I was too scared to use them. "I didn't bring it with me, if that's what you mean," I said. "Just ask Cindy. We found it in her barn."

"I know where you 'found' it, but the question is, how did it get there in the first place?" He kept looking at me like he expected me to break down and confess under the pressure of his "steely gaze," but he finally shrugged.

"Just watch it," he said. "Just watch your step while you're in my territory, that's all." Then he went back to the others like I didn't exist any-more.

Finally it was all over. A tow truck had showed

up and Homer and Alice had gone with it. Sheriff K was standing by his car giving me one final suspicious look when Corie moved a little closer to him. "One thing about that bat, Mel . . ." she said, letting the words dangle.

He frowned. "What's that?"

"From what I hear, they travel in flocks. Where there's one, there's bound to be more." She looked up, over his head toward the trees on the other side of the road. "In fact, I was noticing something over there, in that one tree. A shadow or something, and I thought maybe you could check it out."

His eyes widened, and I'd swear he got pale right before my eyes. He didn't look around, he just slouched down and slid inside his car, very fast, and slammed the door.

"If you still see something there tomorrow," he said, speaking through a small crack in the window, "you call, and we'll see what we can do about it."

And he was gone, gravel spitting out from under his tires.

Behind me, Arnie burst out laughing. "That was mean, Corie, just plain mean. You *know* he's scared to death of anything that flies and is bigger'n a moth."

Corie shrugged and grinned. "I'll be darned.

Would you believe I forgot all about that little phobia of his?"

As you might expect, I had some trouble getting to sleep that night, but once I did, I only woke up once. At least I think that's all. The way I sleep, though, I can't always be sure. Mom says I get up and raid the refrigerator every month or so, and I never know a thing about it, except for a funny taste in my mouth in the morning, and maybe some crumbs in bed.

This time, though, I sort of remembered waking up, but it wasn't all that clear. I thought at first the dream itself had woke me up. I'd been dreaming about the UFO, of course, only now it had gotten a lot bigger and it was kidnapping horses instead of dogs and cats, and the horses were whinnying a lot. But then, after I'd been more or less awake for a few seconds, I heard the horses whinnying for real, a long way off. Probably on the Barker place, I thought, which was off to the north a half mile. The Barkers, Joe and his daughter Betty, were the only ones in the neighborhood who had any horses, so far as I know.

I drifted back to sleep, though, before I could do any more thinking, and the same dream started up again, only now it wasn't a UFO that was picking the horses up. It was a giant bat with a thirty-foot wingspread and it was picking the horses up in its claws and flying away. Only before it got out of sight, I could see that the horse wasn't really a horse. It was a huge can of fruit cocktail, which the bat promptly dropped on the road in front of Corie's house, the way sea gulls drop clams on rocks to break them open.

The last thing I remember is the bat coming in for a landing in the top of the tree Corie'd pointed out to Sheriff K. It just hung there upside down, slurping up the tons of fruit cocktail that had spilled out of the broken can.

7

"Psst! Can You Understand Me?"

I had even less success than usual trying to sleep late the next morning, and I ended up sharing a mostly silent breakfast with Arnie, who wasn't all that happy or rested. Apparently the horse noises had been real, and Arnie was a much lighter sleeper than I was. Corie, who could probably sleep through a mugging, hadn't heard a thing.

Once Arnie left for work, however, Corie and I settled down to ask each other a ton of questions about what the heck was going on. Unfortunately, we only had about an ounce of answers between us.

For instance: Why was the UFO hanging around out here in the woods? Was the light itself a UFO, or was it just the pilot out for a stroll? And if it was just the pilot out riding around in his glowmobile, where was the UFO itself, the mother-ship? But most of all, why did it have such weird-looking things floating around inside it?

Corie, at least, had an idea about that last problem, a sort of elegantly simple idea. You saw what you were thinking about. I'd been thinking about the imaginary Major Corby, and sure enough, there he was. Alice Diefenbacher had been thinking about her dead Aunt May. And Barlow—well, thinking about something with flapping wings and red eyes wouldn't be all that unlikely for him.

"See?" Corie had said at one point. "That would explain a *lot* of UFO sightings, not just these. It would explain why they're all so different from one another. People see what they expect to see. And hardly any two people expect to see the same thing, so they don't."

To tell the truth, the idea sort of "felt right," but the problem was, we couldn't think of any decent reasons for the UFOs to act that way unless they were just trying to confuse the heck out of us, in which case they were a rousing success. The scary part, though, was that, in order to make us "see what we were thinking about," the UFO itself had to have the power to see what we were thinking—to read our minds, in other words. And if you don't think that's scary, just remember some of the things you've thought about now and then, and then imagine them hanging right up there in the air for everyone to see.

Around ten o'clock, though, we wrapped up our guessing games, at least for the moment, and went over to Cindy's place to have another look at the bat. For one thing, Corie was worried about whether it was eating its fruit cocktail yet. Also, after all the wild ideas we'd been kicking around, we couldn't help but wonder if the fact that the bat had showed up within twenty-four hours of the UFO wasn't just too much of a coincidence.

As it turned out, though, we didn't get much more than a glance. When we got to the Engle place, Cindy's father was loading bat and carrier gingerly into his car. Cindy, when her final objection was ignored and the bat was on its way, explained. Her mother had decided, basically, that the bat had to go, whether it ate its fruit cocktail or not, and then Neal Loftus had located a zoo that was willing to take it off our hands, provided it could be delivered. He had even volunteered to do the delivering himself, since he was going to be driving up to the city on business in the afternoon anyway. Mr. Engle was doing his part by delivering the bat to Neal. All of which meant, scratch Cindy's hopes of being a small-town, mosquito-weight P. T. Barnum.

Corie and I were trying to take Cindy's mind off her shattered career by telling her about the UFO's latest escapades when we heard a horse. It was whinnying just like the ones last night, but this time it was a lot closer than the Barker place. In fact, it sounded like it was just over the hill back of the house, where Barlow's Christmas trees started.

We all ran outside while I gave Cindy a quick rundown on last night's horse serenade. And sure enough, when we made it over the fences and to the top of the hill, there was the horse. It was pretty much of a mess, mud all over its legs and tail, sort of like Wildwood Flower, only bigger and not as noisy.

After a few seconds, though, none of us was looking at the horse, or listening to it, either. There was something else out there, coming along behind and to one side of the horse.

The sun was shining, so the thing didn't glow the way it had last night, any more than the moon would glow in the daytime. Instead, it looked like a ball of mist, a roundish chunk of fog floating along silently.

It was the UFO, disguised as a mistball, and it was heading right toward us!

The thing that really amazes me is that not a one of us ran. Maybe we were all frozen solid, or maybe the mistball projected a force field, or who knows—maybe we were just more curious than we were scared.

Anyway, whatever the reason, we stood our ground, and when the mistball got within a dozen or so yards, we could see that something was swirling around inside the mist, but this time nothing solid formed, at least not long enough for us to see it clearly. There *may* have been a flicker of the Major, and maybe something from a monster movie I'd seen on TV a few weeks ago, but nothing stuck around long enough to introduce itself or even be recognized.

Up this close, too, I realized that I could see right through the mistball—trees and fences and everything. They were sort of fuzzy-looking, but they were there. I even started wondering if maybe the Major and the rest were from some kind of projector—you know, an image projected onto a mistball instead of onto a screen. Or maybe the mistball itself was a projection.

Finally, when the thing got within a couple of yards and was almost completely stopped, I heard the same little hissing I'd heard that night with Barlow. A hissing, like a slow leak in a tire, or maybe a teakettle. Was there something solid down there slithering along through the grass, I wondered, throwing up this cloud of mist like a spray can? An aerosol UFO, for crying out loud? What would they think of next?

Then it zapped me.

At least that's what Corie told me later. There was a crackling sound, she said, like an electrical spark, an odd smell for a second, and then I was gone. Literally. She'd been hanging onto my arm, she said, and all of a sudden her hand was empty. Then the mistball "solidified" a little—at least she couldn't see through it quite as easily as before— and it drifted away, back the way it had come.

As for me—well, I haven't the foggiest idea what really happened. I guess I must've been inside the mistball somehow. All I know is, one second I was standing out there in the field, and the next second I was standing in a little room with nothing but bare metal walls. One wall looked a little smoother than the others, but that was the only difference I could see. And the mistball was in one corner, doing a lot of flickering. Or maybe it was a different mistball. It's hard to tell one mistball from another.

The really crazy thing is, I wasn't all that scared, and I wondered again if the mistball was doing something to keep me from going bananas. Or maybe I was just numb, I don't know.

I *was* curious, though, and finally I started looking around. But that didn't take very long. I mean, how long can you take to look over a ten-foot metal cube with a mistball in one corner?

After a while, my curiosity started changing to worry. For one thing, nothing was happening. The least I'd expected was some sort of welcoming committee. *Something.* Unless the mistball *was* the welcoming committee, in which case it was doing a lousy job.

Then I tried talking. "Is anybody there? Who are you? What are you going to do with me?" Basic stuff like that.

But nobody answered, and that's the one time I really got scared. I remembered a story I'd read a couple of years ago, in one of those "golden age" science-fiction anthologies. Some people were picked up by an alien spaceship or something, and they were all dumped into a room a lot like this one. What they had to do to get out was prove they were intelligent. And for the life of me— maybe literally—I couldn't remember how they'd proved it.

I did a little wall pounding about then, which got me absolutely nothing but a bruise on one hand.

Finally, though, something started happening. There was a sound. Not a voice, just a faint, un-even hissing, like someone whispering, or maybe saying "Psst!" over and over. It wasn't much, but it was a big improvement over the total silence.

Needless to say, I started asking my basic questions all over again, loudly, but it didn't seem to make any difference.

Then the noise started getting louder but not any clearer, like someone had a radio tuned off to one side of a station and he turned the volume up instead of changing the tuning. It was still all mushy sounding, but now at least it was loud mush.

Then all of a sudden it was even louder, so loud I was surprised my ears didn't hurt, the way they had at that rock concert last year. At the same time, the noise turned into words, like someone shouting right in my ear. And they were the same words, over and over:

"Can you understand me? Can you understand me? Can you . . ."

And the voice sounded scared, a lot more scared than I was.

Then it started to fade, like someone messing with the tuning again, and I managed to yell: "I understand you!"

Silence. Total silence, except for my own heart beating and the mistball hissing a little. This was it, I thought. This was it.

Communication had been established.

I was about to learn the secrets of the Universe and God knows what else!

8

"Are You the Dominant Life Form?"

But it didn't work that way. I realized pretty fast that I wasn't going to learn the secrets of the Universe or much of anything else.

All that voice wanted to do was *ask* questions, which was just plain silly. I mean, people—or things—that cruise around in UFOs and snatch perfect strangers up out of Christmas tree fields in broad daylight are supposed to *answer* questions, not ask them.

Oh, I tried. Believe me, I tried, but it just didn't do any good.

"Who are you?" I asked.

"Are you the dominant life form?" it asked right back.

"Where are you from?" I asked.

"What level is your civilization?" it asked.

"Why are you here?" I asked.

"Have you isolated all the elements?" it asked.

"Are there more of you on earth?" I asked.

"Can you understand me?" it asked, and all of a sudden the volume went up again, getting so loud I put my hands over my ears.

And that's when I realized it wasn't a voice at all. Putting my hands over my ears didn't have any effect at all. The voice was just as loud as before. Therefore the voice wasn't a voice, it was some sort of telepathy, right?

But if it was telepathy, why was he—it?—asking all these questions? Why wasn't he just reading my mind instead of messing around this way?

"CAN YOU UNDERSTAND ME?" It was back again, and it sounded really frantic.

"Yes!" I yelled back. "But hold it down a little, huh?" My head was starting to ache.

"YOU *CAN* UNDERSTAND ME?" Still loud and frantic.

"I told you, yes! But not so loud!"

A hesitation, and then: "Can you still understand me?" Still loud, but at least it wasn't threatening to turn my brain to Jello any second.

"Yes," I said. "That's a little better. Now who are—"

"Are you a member of the dominant life form?"

Back to that again. I'd never find out *anything* this way, let alone the secrets of the Universe.

"All right!" I said. "I guess you could say I am. Now who—"

"Are you familiar with the elements?" Still nervous sounding.

"What elements?"

Another brief silence. "The chemical elements. Such as oxygen, which the life forms on this planet breathe. Such as nitrogen, which is also present in your atmosphere."

He was starting to sound like my chemistry teacher last year. "I know some of them," I said. "And I've seen a periodic table." It started with hydrogen in the upper left corner and worked its way down to Fermium or Lawrencium or whatever the latest and heaviest artificial element was. And there were a *lot* of elements in between, very few of which I could remember.

"Good," the voice said. "You must bring me five pounds of—of . . ."

Now what? I wondered as the voice stuttered to a halt. "Five pounds of what?" I asked.

"An element." The voice was starting to sound panicky again.

"What element?"

"I do not know! Its name can not be identified

in your mind!" Sheer panic now. What kind of UFO *was* this? *I'm* the one who's supposed to be panicked, not the pilot. But, then, I'm the one who's supposed to be asking questions, too, but that wasn't going according to the script, either.

"Is something wrong?" I asked.

"If the element is not brought to me, we will all be destroyed! This ship is damaged! If it is not repaired, it will explode! And it cannot be repaired unless it is given the right element!"

Which was reason enough to be panicky, I guess. "So you want me to bring you this element," I began, but the voice cut me off.

"It must be brought to the *ship!* The ship will make use of it. I could not— The element *must* be brought!"

"*What* element?" I asked again, as calmly as I could, which wasn't all that calm now. Compared to the voice, though, I was still pretty much in control. But, then, anything short of screaming and pounding my head against the wall would've been calm compared to the voice. "Maybe if you tell me what element you need, I can find it for you."

"I can only identify it by—by its weight! And you do not *know* the weights of the elements!"

"I know hydrogen has a weight of one. And uranium is two-thirty-five. Or maybe two-thirty-eight. There's more than one kind."

"It is neither of those! The one the ship needs is —it is approximately two hundred seven times as massive as hydrogen. But you do not have knowledge of—"

"I can find out, for crying out loud!" There's nothing like having an hysterical UFO pilot on your hands. To tell the truth, though, I think having to try to calm him down helped keep *me* more or less calm. "If you let me out of here," I went on, "I can look it up in my chemistry book. You *are* going to let me out, aren't you?"

Another silence, and I could almost feel the indecision. In fact, maybe I *could* feel it.

"You will come back?" the voice asked.

"If I can. I didn't 'come' here in the first place. Which reminds me—how *did* I get here?"

"You were brought by the mistball."

"The mistball? You mean *you* call it that, too?"

"Call it what? There must be something wrong. That did not translate properly. Can you understand me?" Back to that again, along with more panic.

"But you just—" I stopped and began again. "Look, there are about a million things I want to know. If I bring this element back, *then* will you answer my questions?"

"Yes! Anything! But— Are there others of your life form nearby?"

Others of my life form . . . "There's a town a few miles away," I said. "Or I think there is. Where am I right now?" For all I knew, I could be on the moon.

"We are approximately a half mile from where you were picked up by the mistball."

Which would put us back in the woods, I thought, around the swamp if the wet livestock was any indication. "There's a collection of three or four thousand people—my life form—four or five miles from here," I said.

"Can you visualize how to get there?"

"More or less. But why—"

"Do so."

So I did. The voice seemed a little calmer then, and I thought I felt the room move a little. And I had a minute or so to think.

"Look," I said, "if you're so worried about me not being able to identify the element, why don't you just send the mistball out to pick up someone else? Or lots of someone elses? Come to think of it, why can't it just pick up the element itself?"

"The mistball is not designed to work that way. It cannot be controlled."

"But it—"

"It can only pick up random samples of life

forms on a planet. That is what it is designed to do. I have no control over what it selects. All I can do is reject the samples it brings in so that it will have to continue bringing in more. I rejected many samples before it finally brought you. You are the first sample I have been able to communicate with."

Rejecting samples . . . "You picked up a cat? And a dog? A horse?"

"Yes, those are some I rejected. They could not communicate."

"And a bat?"

"That was from a previous collection point on another part of your world, before the ship was damaged. But we are wasting time! I have caused the ship to move where you directed. If I release you, can you send others of your life form to me?"

"*Send* someone? In here?" It didn't take a lot of imagination to see what sort of reaction I'd get to something like that: *Would you care to step into this flying saucer, sir? No? Well, I didn't think so, but I just thought I'd ask. And really, sir, why are you laughing?*

I'd be lucky if all they did was laugh. "No," I said, "I don't think I'd be able to send anyone back in here. But I already told you, *I* can find out what the element is myself. All I have to do is look up the weight you gave me."

Another nervous silence, and then: "Very well. I seem to have no choice."

"All right. Now, how do I get out of here? And if I do find the element—"

"You must!"

"All right, all right! I believe you. But how do I get back in here if you can't order your mistball to pick me up again?"

"I will leave the door open."

The simplest solutions are the best. Why didn't *I* think of that? "You'd better be careful who you let in, though. And another thing—you better keep your mistball inside until I come back."

"But why? It can be bringing more samples. Perhaps another—"

"Look, in case you didn't know it, that thing scares people half to death."

"Scares them? But I do not understand. It produces images of what is in the minds of the life forms it approaches." So Corie had been right! "How can they be frightened of images from their own minds? It is intended to calm them, not frighten them."

I thought for a second about trying to explain about ghost stories and horror movies and imaginary invasions from outer space, but I got the feeling he wouldn't have the faintest idea what I was talking about.

"Take my word for it," I said. "Incidentally, how long until your ship blows up? And how big an explosion will it be?"

A short silence, and then: "Eleven of your hours. And it will vaporize approximately two cubic miles."

For once the voice sounded businesslike, as if it were just reading off statistics, but this time I came close to panicking myself. Eleven hours! And if a couple of cubic *miles* were going to be *vaporized* . . . The biggest hydrogen bomb in the world couldn't come anywhere *near* doing something like that!

Up until then, I have to admit I'd been having occasional thoughts of just bugging out in case I couldn't find the element he needed. I'd thought I could get everyone away from the ship, and then just bug out. But *two cubic miles!* There was no way to bug out far enough. That would wipe out half the country, at the very least . . .

Then, while I was still being dumbfounded, one of the metal walls vanished and sunlight poured in. Through the opening, I could see a stone lion on a pedestal, and I realized the UFO had *really* come down in the middle of town. It was right on the court house lawn, no less. A dozen people were standing on the steps around the lion and another dozen were on the grass. They looked scared. But no sound was coming through, and I could see a faint, wavering in the air right where the wall had been.

"Can't you just move the ship somewhere else?" I yelled. "Somewhere in orbit? Then you can come back to pick up this element when—"

"No! That would only make it happen sooner! One hour was already lost by moving the ship to this location. Now go! And remember—*two hundred seven!*"

"I'll remember!" Provided I don't faint when I get out of here, that is.

I waited another second and then stepped through the "door" and dropped the two feet to the court house lawn. It was like going through some kind of invisible curtain. Until that very second, there hadn't been a sound, but now there was more racket than I knew what to do with. It was all over me. People were yelling. Sirens were going. Horns were honking. And over everything else was the town's civil defense siren, which was just a hundred feet up in the court house tower. You could hear it a couple miles away, at least, so when you were right under it like this, you could *really* hear it.

I'd barely touched the ground when I realized just how much trouble we were in. Inside, where everything had been quiet, I had known that putting the UFO down in the middle of town had not been a good idea. But out here, in the midst of the real world, it all suddenly became very, very clear that "not a good idea" was putting it mildly. It had been a *lousy* idea! Not only was nobody going to calmly wander into the UFO's open door, nobody would even be *allowed* into the UFO. In fact, *I* wouldn't be allowed back in, whether I was able to find the element the ship needed or not. Just like in the movies, the UFO would be "sealed off," especially to some smart-aleck kid from the city like me.

And then . . .

9

"That Wasn't Any Kid!
That Was One of Them!"

All that realizing didn't take long. It all hit me about the same time my feet hit the ground. Instant realization or something like that. And for once in my life, I followed up with instant action.

Practically the second I hit the ground, I made a fast turn and ran like crazy around to the other side of the UFO. The people around the stone lion had gotten a quick look at me, but the ones on the other side hadn't, so for all they knew, I was just some nutty kid who'd run up to the UFO on the other side and was now getting away before it zapped me. At least I hoped they'd think that long enough for me to disappear into the crowd.

And would you believe it? It worked!

I made it across the lawn and all the way into the crowd that had already collected along Main

80

"All right, settle down, all of you!" the sheriff snapped. "Now Barlow, what's this got to do with you?"

Barlow shrugged and grinned. "Russ here's a buddy of mine, that's all. Besides, he was standin' right next to me when that thing come down, so I sure don't see how he coulda' been inside it like Estel says."

Sheriff K turned his eyes on me. He was scowling. "That right, Nelson?"

I didn't trust myself to say anything, so I just nodded. Sheriff K kept staring at me.

"All right, Nelson," he said finally, "I don't know what's going on here, but I don't have time to fool with you now. But I want to have a talk with you and that cousin of yours when this thing is settled. So don't you go heading back to that big city of yours without letting me know."

He turned back to the UFO and stalked off through the crowd with only a quick glance toward Estel, who looked very unhappy as he jerked around and trailed after the sheriff.

"See?" Barlow cackled. "I told you you was with me all the time."

10

"So Much for Goin' Public!"

To cut a long story short, I finally found—or was found by—Corie and Cindy (they'd more or less followed the giant garbage can lid into town). From then on, though, the day was just one disaster after another.

We found the lead—in the form of a couple of twenty-pound lead paperweights Corie remembered from when she'd worked at the *Tribune*—but they didn't do us or the UFO a lot of good. By the time we got them—one for me and one for Barlow—Sheriff K was not only getting things organized, he was starting to sound downright possessive. He kept calling it "my saucer," and he wasn't about to let *anyone* get close to it, at least not until the "proper authorities" arrived, whoever they might turn out to be. And to back him up, he'd managed to get just about every cop and deputy in the county lined up around the saucer. There was even

talk about getting a truck full of National Guardsmen, provided Mayor Hartlerode could convince
Governor Borden that he (Hartlerode) was not either (*a*) crazy, or (*b*) trying to get into the
Guinness Book of World Records by pulling the
biggest practical joke since Orson Welles invaded
New Jersey.

In short, it was hopeless, and then, around four,
it got worse. The National Guard actually arrived
and surrounded the UFO, complete with sawhorse
barricades and rifles. Then the TV types started
showing up around six, which at least made Sheriff K happy. He managed to get on all three networks by seven, and by seven-thirty he was
"denying rumors" that his friends were planning to
draft him to run for governor in the fall.

Somewhere in there, we talked to Cindy's par-
ents, hoping they might have some idea how one
of us might make it into the UFO, but they didn't.
Corie even tried talking to Sheriff K himself once,
hoping he might be reasonable for a change. No
such luck, of course. Before she could even *try*
telling him anything, he was telling her that she
had better just butt out and "that goes for that
twerp cousin of yours, too!" *He* was in charge, and
that was that, and if he thought I'd really been inside that thing, the way Estel said, he'd lock me
and Corie and Barlow up on the spot.

"But what if he'd found out something important in there?" Corie asked, standing up to his glare. "Something really important!"

"I'll decide what's important, young lady!" He sounded like he was still ticked off about the bat episode last night. "And don't think any of you can pull the wool over my eyes, either! I know all about those trashy books you write, so I know you're good at dreaming up all sorts of crazy things. Just don't try it with *me!*"

And that was definitely that.

Then Arnie showed up and convinced the Engles that the whole thing was just a big publicity stunt. "Sure, it's another of those schlock outfits trying to make an imitation *Close Encounters,* and they got themselves a big budget and their PR men went crazy. Just wait'll the networks get a big enough audience, around nine or ten tonight! That thing'll light up like a neon sign, and *then* we'll find out who's really behind it."

And he didn't think much of my saucer-in-distress story, either. "Come on, Russ! How could a race advanced enough to have interstellar travel let one of their ships get into a pickle like that?"

That last remark, though, got a fast cackle from Barlow, who was surprising me more every time he opened his mouth. "Just 'cause they got a lot of science don't mean they necessarily got good sense. Or that they got everything all figured out. Look what happened to those guys on the way to the moon a few years back. Apollo Thirteen, wasn't it? Blooey! They just barely made it back home. And then there was that other one, where the fender fell off their little electric car while they was right up there on the moon. Remember?"

But it didn't help. Arnie just laughed and said he'd catch the last act on the ten o'clock news. Then the Engles left, practically dragging Cindy, so our little army of lead paperweight haulers was down to three.

About eight, things got even worse. The mistball came out and it was glowing again. It hovered by the door for a few seconds, as if it couldn't make up its mind what to do, then floated across the lawn to the southwest. It was almost up to the circle of guardsmen when something appeared in the middle of it. It wasn't Major Corby or even a leathery-winged demon. In a way, it was worse.

It was Gort—you know, the seven-foot robot in *Day the Earth Stood Still.*

I heard Corie laugh, a sound that sort of stood out among the shrieks. "No wonder!" she said, leaning toward me and Barlow. "That movie was on the late show just last Saturday!"

The mistball kept going, and the crowd, including the guardsmen, parted like a panicky Red Sea.

A couple of empty beer cans came flying out of the crowd on one side and went right through the mistball and into the crowd on the other side. The people on the receiving end just started yelling all the louder, probably because they figured the mistball was throwing strange looking grenades at them.

But the mistball—and Gort—ignored everything and plowed ahead.

"I thought your buddy was gonna keep that thing inside," Barlow said.

"He was, but he's probably getting worried. He's only got three hours or so to go, and I still haven't gotten back in there." Worried was an understatement, I thought. He was probably totally out of his mind, and I couldn't blame him.

The mistball did give Corie an idea, though. If we couldn't think of anything better by around ten, when we'd have only an hour to go, we would try an all-out assault at the same time the mistball made one of its appearances. Corie, who didn't have a paperweight, would make as much uproar as she could. Then Barlow, with his own paperweight, would make a dash—or a shamble— through the guardsmen, and then, when everyone was, we hoped, watching and catching Corie and Barlow, I'd have a chance to take *my* paperweight through in the midst of all the confusion.

Unfortunately, around nine-thirty, our opening act got picked up. Some guy with a microphone and a video camera was wandering around the crowd interviewing the natives, and he picked Corie. Sheriff K must've been watching the monitors, because she'd only gotten a couple sentences out—unfavorable sentences from his viewpoint, I'm sure—when he showed up and waved the interviewer away. Then he talked at Corie for a minute, and from a distance it looked like he was saying the same things he'd said earlier, only this time he *did* haul her away.

Barlow and I did our best to melt into the crowd as Corie was led off by an apologetic-looking deputy.

"So much for goin' public," Barlow said after a minute. "Guess it's just up to us now."

11

"Bein' Blowed Up Scares
Me a Lot More!"

And so it was. Up to the two of us, that is. The only trouble was, we didn't have any idea what to do.

"Guess we better just take our best shot, huh?" Barlow said a few minutes later, when the court house clock clanged ten times.

I shivered a little. "I guess so. Unless you have a better idea . . . ?"

Barlow shrugged. "I can do a lot of screamin' and hollerin', but I sure ain't gonna be able to make it all the way up to that thing myself. Them guys is fast."

I nodded, remembering a couple of kids the guardsmen had already caught. They'd been moving a lot faster than I ever could, weighted down

like I was with my twenty pounds of lead. Barlow might be able to kick up a pretty good storm, but I couldn't see him raising enough of a racket to give me time to stumble across a hundred feet of open lawn.

The mistball came back about then, complete with Gort, of course.

"Too bad you can't talk to your buddy inside there," Barlow said, watching the mistball. "Maybe you could get him to help out a little. Maybe get him to change the show."

I looked at him blankly.

"You know," he said. "Old tin britches there is gettin' sort of old hat. Ever'one's used to him. Now if he'd come up with somethin' different, like maybe that critter he was showin' to *me* before you showed up that first time. . . ." He cackled again, but I had the feeling he was just putting it on, trying to relax me "That thing'd scare the daylights out of 'em, all right."

My blank stare lasted another half second, and then I remembered: The thing with the wings and the tail and the glowing eyes that had been behind the Major inside the mistball. I also remembered something else with wings and a tail—the bat.

The bat!

All of a sudden my heart was thumping, and I thought: Maybe we *do* have a chance!

We were in luck. Neal Loftus was still in the *Tribune* office. He had three miniature TV sets going, one for each network, but he wasn't watching any of them. He was standing looking out the big front window toward the court house, talking into a cassette recorder.

More important, though, the bat was still there. He'd forgotten all about it, *and* about his trip, which wasn't all that surprising, considering what was going on across the street.

After I explained why we needed the bat, he just looked at Barlow. "Do *you* believe him?" he asked.

"I ain't positive, but I figure we can't hardly afford to take a chance," Barlow said, grinning crookedly. "And you can come along and take pictures," he added. "Pictures none of them TV guys will know are gonna happen."

I guess that tipped the scales. We got the bat.

Unfortunately, once Barlow got a look at the carrier, he started having doubts. "Sure, it'd cause a lot of commotion if you dump it out right in front of that crowd, but look't the way it's hangin' on. You really think it *can* be dumped?"

He was right. I remembered the way we had to cut the extension cord to get it into the bag in the first place. If the bat decided to hang onto the cage, "dumping" it would be easier said than done. And even getting the cat carrier through the crowd didn't look all that easy, now that I thought about it.

I guess Barlow saw the look on my face.

"Hold on a minute," he said, "just hold on a minute. Don't think you're the only one who c'n get an idea now and then. Maybe I could carry the critter by itself."

I guess I just looked blank.

"I mean," he went on, "I saw a picture of one of them critters once. Wings all spread out and everything. Some character who didn't know no better was holdin' the wings, holdin' 'em all spread out." Barlow spread his own arms wide to demonstrate.

I blinked. *"You'd* be willing to try something like that? I thought bats scared you."

"They do. But bein' blowed up scares me a lot more!"

"But you don't really *know* it's going to explode. All you've got—"

"All I've got's your word. You sayin' it *ain't* gonna blow up? You been foolin' us all day?"

"No! I just thought you—"

"Well, you just stop thinkin' for me. Now *is* it gonna blow up? Or ain't it?"

"I *think* it is. I mean, he—it *told* me it would, and—"

"Okay, then. He oughta' know, right?"

So that was that. Barlow opened the cat carrier and poked at the bat with his finger until it spread its wings. Then, somehow, he managed to get hold of them. He made a lot of faces, but he hung on while Neal and I shifted the carrier and pried the bat's claws loose. It twitched and squealed at first, but eventually it quieted down. To tell the truth, I felt like twitching and squealing myself. If I'd been Barlow, I never could've hung onto the thing like that, explosion or no explosion.

Anyway, after a minute or two, Barlow was holding the bat out in front of him, all spread out and unhappy. The body didn't look so big now, but the wings more than made up for it.

"You get on out there," Barlow said, "right up front and ready to run. When old tin britches shows up again, me'n Dracula here'll come out and start our own little ruckus." He cackled happily, probably thinking about the reactions he'd get when he plowed through the crowd with the bat in front of him.

So I took my paperweight and, followed by Neal, worked my way through the crowd once again. Neal kept up a running commentary into the microphone he'd clipped to his collar so he'd have his hands free for the camera.

We didn't have long to wait. I'd been at the barricades only a couple of minutes when the mistball showed up about a block away. I glanced back toward the *Tribune*, and there was Barlow, backing out the door with the bat.

As for me, *everything* was acting up. My stomach was twitching, my heart was making my shirt buttons bounce, and my armpits felt like swamps. I was shaking so much I could barely hang onto the chunk of lead.

Then, when I turned back toward the saucer, a great big sinking feeling was added to everything else. Sheriff K had popped up from somewhere and was standing right in front of me. He gave the two nearest guardsmen a quick "I've got everything under control" look and then glared at me.

"All right, Nelson, just what are you and that cousin of yours up to? And where's Hunneshagen? I've been keeping an eye on you all day. Now if you don't want me to haul *you* in like I did your cousin, you just give me a few answers! And I mean answers I can believe!"

The best I could do was a shaky "I don't know what you're talking about." It didn't help.

"Don't give me that! I don't know what's going

on yet, but— You *were* the one Estel saw coming out of that thing, weren't you? *Weren't you?*" He reached out and grabbed one of my arms, and that's when he noticed the lead.

"And what, pray tell, is *that?*" he asked, pointing.

Would you believe I asked, "What is what?" I was pretty much a total shambles at that point.

"That—that *lump* in your right hand!" he snapped.

Luckily, I didn't have to answer, because right about then some people in another part of the crowd started screaming. Barlow and the bat were on their way, I thought, but how much good was it going to do as long as Sheriff K was hanging onto my arm like an anchor?

"Get over there and see what's going on," Sheriff K snapped to the nearest guardsman, who trotted off obediently. Meanwhile, the hand on my arm only got tighter.

By that time, the mistball—with Gort in the middle, as usual—was almost to the front of the crowd, and so was the bubble of commotion around Barlow. Sheriff K was craning and stretching, trying to see what was causing this new ruckus, but he still wasn't letting go of my arm.

Then the Barlow bubble reached the front of the crowd and he popped out behind the barricades maybe seventy-five feet around the circle from me and Sheriff K. The comments were flying thick and fast all around me.

"Who's that? Some drunk?"

"It's Hunneshagen, ain't it?"

"Looks that way, but what's that thing he's got?"

"Looks like a kite." A raucous laugh. "He's *really* flipped out this time! A kite!"

"You sure? It don't look—"

"But why all the noise? What—"

"My God! It's alive!"

"It's a monster! It's—"

And that's when Barlow held the bat way out in front of himself, gave it a toss, and let go.

It flapped clumsily for a second, caught itself, then swooped toward the ground like it was trying to get up speed, and then flapped up and over the head of one of the guardsmen, who promptly dropped his rifle and fell to the ground, covering his head with his arms. By then, the bat was ten or fifteen feet in the air and starting to flap in a circle. Practically everyone was yelling or screaming or ducking or all three.

And that's when I heard the loudest scream of all, practically in my ear. It was Sheriff K, and at the same time he screamed, just when the bat made a swerve in our direction, he let go of my arm.

It took me a second to realize I could move

again and that I had someplace to move to. Like everyone else, I'd forgotten everything except for some occasional breathing.

Anyway, I tore my eyes away from the bat and ducked under the barricade and started running—almost staggering, what with the weight of the lead and the fact that my arm was numb from where Sheriff K had been clutching it like a tourniquet.

Nobody *seemed* to be paying any attention to me. At least no one grabbed at me that I could feel, and I was beginning to think I was going to make it, if I didn't fall down or drop the lead.

But then, over all the other racket. I heard shots. They were coming from right behind me, too, so loud they drowned out all the shouting and screaming.

I guess I screamed myself, and I either jumped or fell flat on my face on the grass, fully expecting to be shot dead the next instant by a fanatic guard or maybe a frantic Sheriff K.

But as soon as I hit the ground, I managed to look back. It was Sheriff K who was doing the shooting, all right, but he wasn't shooting at me!

He was shooting at the bat!

And the two nearest guardsmen were grabbing him and wrestling his gun away from him. They weren't looking at *me*, not any of them!

I scrambled to my feet and ran, fell down, managed to get up again, and finally made it to the door of the UFO. I tossed the lead through and dived in after it.

Five or ten seconds later, while I was still lying panting and sweating on the floor, the mistball—without Gort—floated calmly in behind me.

The door closed.

12

"See, I Told You So!"

And that, more or less, was that.

By the time I recovered enough to stand up, the voice was tuning in on me again, telling me to put the lead over in one corner. I did, and it promptly disappeared. I think it fell through the floor, but I'm not sure. Anyway, it was gone, and some sort of uneven humming started up.

Then I started asking questions again.

I didn't get any answers this time, either. All I got was a "feeling," like the panicky feeling I'd picked out of the air the first time I'd been in here. The pilot—or whatever he was—was there, all right, but he wasn't saying anything. Maybe he was just waiting to see how the lead worked out.

Anyway, after a few minutes, all the panic sort of evaporated, and all of a sudden I felt like letting my breath out in a huge sigh of relief, which is, I guess, what the voice was doing, mentally.

102

Then I felt the ship move, just like it had the other time.

"Wait a minute!" I yelled, and suddenly I remembered what the voice had said this morning about picking up random samples of life forms. For a zoo back home? Experiments? Or what?

"WAIT A MINUTE!" All the questions I'd been trying to get answered were gone from my head. All I could think was that I'd saved his hide and now he was going to kidnap me! Which, I suppose, just goes to show that I'm as paranoid as the next guy if the situation calls for it.

"It is all right," the voice said. "I am returning you to your original location."

"You're not taking me back with you?"

"Of course not. We are not allowed to keep a member of any species that has developed a language—unless that member is willing." A pause. "Are you willing to be taken to my planet?"

For about a half second, a hundred stories of interstellar empires and trips to other worlds rattled around in my head. But in the next half second, I saw all kinds of creepy, crawly creatures and poisonous atmospheres and cages in a zoo, and I yelled: "No! No, I'm not willing!"

"Very well," the voice said. "I will return you to your original location."

I was silent for a moment, feeling limp. Then I tried my questions again.

But I still didn't get any worthwhile answers. For one thing, I didn't have much time. For another, the voice didn't know very many answers— or so it said. For instance, "I have no idea where I come from in relation to your planet. The ship knows. I do not." Or, "I have no idea how the ship's drive works. I am not a scientist."

And what few answers he did try to give came out half gibberish. They just did not translate, apparently, just like *lead* hadn't translated before. Nothing the ship could find in my mind quite fit what the voice was trying to say. For instance, "I am about three feet wide and—" ended in complete nonsense, the same as "The life form samples will be put in a—" When I said "Zoo?" the voice said, "That did not translate properly," so there we were.

And so it went, for all of three or four minutes, at which point I guess the mistball got tired of waiting for me to jump out the door. Whatever happened, the little metal room vanished all of a sudden, and the next thing I knew, I was standing in the middle of Barlow's pine trees—my "original location." The mistball was floating back toward the UFO, which still looked like a giant garbage can lid, even in the moonlight. The mistball went inside, the door closed, and the whole thing zipped straight up without a sound. It was out of sight in a couple of seconds.

So much for first contact with an alien civilization.

Everything else, like my unanswered questions, was an anticlimax. There was just enough moonlight for me to find my way over the hill and down to the Engle place, where Cindy and her folks had been watching the UFO on TV until it had taken off a few minutes before. Only one of the networks was still carrying the story, and its reporters and commentators were sounding unhappy.

Cindy, of course, wanted to know what had happened to me, and once I told her, she told me what had happened back in town after I managed to get inside the UFO—which action the networks had all missed, by the way. They had all been watching either the mistball or the bat or Sheriff K going into hysterics.

First, the UFO took off, which I'd already guessed, but about five minutes later a whole fleet of PR men showed up, towing the gorgeous, blond star of their soon-to-be-released movie, *Invasion from the Stars*. They'd seen the first network pictures on the evening news, and they'd realized—they said—that it was too good an opportunity to miss, so they'd chartered a jet and headed straight for Farwell. Unfortunately—or fortunately—they hadn't quite made it by the time the UFO took off.

"Looks like Arnie was right," Mr. Engle had said when the blonde first showed up, and now he repeated it for my benefit. I don't know how he thought I'd gotten all the way out to their place so fast if the saucer wasn't real, but it didn't seem to bother him very much. The only thing that bothered Cindy's mother was the "terrible turn" my imagination seemed to have taken.

When the last network went back to regular programming, Mr. Engle insisted on driving me home. All Arnie said when I came in the door was, "See? I told you so."

Corie, who had been released by the deputies about the same time their boss, Sheriff K, had gone bat berserk, showed up a couple minutes later. Barlow was with her, although neither of them was quite sure why, and Arnie wasn't all that happy to see him.

"Guess I'm lucky you didn't bring the blankety-blank bat home, too," he said as he headed for the bedroom. (The bat, incidentally, was found the next day in the court house tower, none the worse for wear. Apparently Sheriff K is not all that great a shot when he is panicked out of his mind.)

Corie and Barlow and I, of course, couldn't even think about sleep, so we sat around talking most of the night. Not that it did any good, but I guess we were just trying to get it all set in our heads, so that, no matter what anyone said later, we would all remember that it had been real.

Anyway, nothing was really settled, though I do remember Barlow coming on pretty strong whenever Corie or I would say anything about "how could anyone bright enough to travel from star to star be so ignorant?" He didn't think it was all that hard to believe, as he had pointed out to Cindy's father earlier.

"Look at *you*," he said, pointing at me and letting go with another minor cackle. "All summer you're gonna be phonin' people, askin' 'em questions, and I bet if somethin' went wrong with that phone you're gonna use, or with that little gadget they got hooked up to it to keep track of the answers, I bet you couldn't fix 'em any better'n your buddy could his saucer."

I frowned, and he cackled again and went on. "S'pose the phone went dead. Or your machine went dead. Could you fix 'em? Or tell anyone how they work?"

"But that's different!"

"Is it?" He didn't cackle, just grinned, and I couldn't help but wonder if maybe he wasn't right.

As the planet and then the star shrank into nothingness behind him, he let out his equivalent of a huge sigh of relief. He was going to make it home after all!

Then, as he settled back into the transport fluid, he began mentally to make a list of resolutions.

Never again would he trust anyone who told him, "Don't worry, it's foolproof!"

Never again would he let himself be sent off-planet without making sure there was someone along who knew how the ship worked, no matter how simple the manufacturer said everything was.

And never again would he take a job like this, no matter how routine and dull they said it would be, not during this or any other vacation, not even after he graduated.

About the Author

GENE DEWEESE has written several adult science-fiction novels and a book on dollmaking. He has also, under a slightly different, name, authored several gothic novels, including *Nightmare in Pewter*. Mr. DeWeese and his wife, a librarian, live in Milwaukee, Wisconsin.